THUG

SHORTS

WAHIDA CLARK PRESENTS PUBLISHING, LLC

Wahida Clark Presents Publishing, LLC
60 Evergreen Place
Suite 904
East Orange, New Jersey 07018
www.wclarkpublishing.com
1 (866) 910-6920

Thug Shorts

ISBN Hardcover: 978-194773212-4

Cover design and layout by Nuance Art LLC

Book interior design by Nuance Art LLC via
www.aCreatveNuance.com

FOREWORD

By Wahida Clark

First and foremost, I would like to thank you so much for your continued support of the Thug series. I decided to write this collection to give you what you want—more drama, insight, and background information on the characters you have grown to love over the years. One thing to note with these shorts, they can only be fully appreciated if you have read the first six *Thug* books in the Thugs and the Women Who Love Them series. For those of you who have read all of the books, here's a quick recap of what set off all the drama.

Previously in *Justify My Thug* . . .

Trae Macklin got caught cheating! And once his wife, Tasha, finds out, all hell breaks loose. Riddled with guilt, Trae pours his heart out in an Apology *Letter* to his wife. But Tasha could care less about Trae's apology and seeks out a fiery *Response* by the name of Kyron. *Shit Just Got Real.* In the meantime, Trae continues piling on the drama of his toxic situations, and Tasha now has to deal with the circumstances of her revenge. When Kyron weighs in and pens a letter back to Tasha, it all explodes!

My goal with these *Shorts* is to take you inside the mind of the characters, allowing for insight into their views and hidden emotions—a way for the readers to fully connect with the characters in a manner that hasn't been previously explored.

It's so crazy to me how much you all have grown to love Kyron! I keep asking myself, what if I hadn't killed him off? I already had scenes outlined with him and Tasha, and in one of the scenes, she had his son and a daughter for Trae, and was trying to juggle both men. However, she was only dealing with Kyron because of their son. Crazy, right? In a nutshell, that is how the *Private Sessions* with Kyron Santos came about. It's the first two of the *Private Sessions* collection.

I hope you enjoy these *Shorts*!

Until next time,
Thuggishly Yours,

Wahida Clark

THE LETTER

By

TRAE MACKLIN

The Boss

Tasha,

I'm not good at apologies, mainly because I rarely get practice since I don't make a lot of mistakes. And that's not me on some conceited shit. Not making mistakes is a truth that helped me avoid death in the streets and make millions in the real world. In the life I live, mistakes can cost me my life and cause a nigga to go broke. So my words are well thought out and I think before I act. Usually.

I have sat and thought long and hard about you. About us. And I realized I strayed from the Trae I use to be. The Trae you fell in love with. The Trae that you committed yourself to. Instead I'm the Trae that fucked up. On the real I don't know how that Trae came into the picture. And I damn sure can't believe I'm keeping it 100 and admitting that I fucked up. Shit, I can't even believe I fucked up the way I did.

They say, "Love will make people do some crazy things." Crazy like me putting my hands on you, something I

1

promised you I would never do. Crazy like me fuckin' that bitch Charli Li another thing I promised I would never do. The thing that hurts me the most was when you said my promises use to be something you could put your life on and now those very same promises, they don't mean shit.

I know this might sound like a copout but being in love with you is the only way I can explain me blowing my cool and fuckin' up. That's not an excuse, it's an explanation. I'm just trying to make sense of all this.

You're probably wondering what the hell am I talking about? How did me loving you make me hurt you? Physically. You know how when people can't find something intelligent to express what they wanna say, they start cursing? It's all emotional and it's the same thing with not having an intelligent way to express your feelings through actions.

Sitting on that plane looking at you glow from carrying the next man's seed and then to add insult to injury, looking at those same lips that use to make my dick hard on sight, you had the nerve to ask about the next nigga. At that moment, I fucking lost it. If I didn't love you so much, it wouldn't have meant nothing to me. But I do. So I was angry. Hurt. Scared to death of the possibility of losing you. I didn't know what to say, what to do. On instinct, before I realized it, I'm choking flames out of you. Fortunately, I caught myself before I lost the only woman I ever loved to my own emotions.

Guess the bottom line of all this is we both fucked up. I

didn't go to sleep and wake up with Charli Li, who you know I don't give a fuck about, in my bed. And we both know you didn't just slip and fall on Kyron's dick. That shit there was payback and I will have to live with the fact that my bullshit pushed you into the arms of another man, which I have to admit I'm still having a hell of time getting over.

When you left you took the best of me with you, REAL TALK!!! Shit, I went to Stephon's funeral just to see you. Ain't that some shit? I'm at a service for somebody's death, and I'm there trying to get my wife and my life back. Guess that's proof I felt like I was dead without you. Ain't no chick never had me open like that. And I ain't talking about pussy. Everything about you is just right. Your smile, your eyes, your laugh, the way you whisper my name when I'm holding you. I was thinking back to when we first met and you use to braid my hair and play hard to get. I loved that shit. I played our song the other day and reminisced about my butterfly. I miss those days. I miss my wife. I miss us. I can't even front.

You have definitely done some shit that makes me mad, no doubt, but even when I'm vexed at you, I can't stop loving you. And I know you feel the same about me.

That's why after all the bullshit we always bounce back. That's why I'm here writing this letter, opening up to you like I would never do, and have never done to another woman. Ain't no flawless relationship, Tash. You need to come to grips with that. I'm trying to make sense of how I made some mistakes and how we can get pass this. In other words, I'm starting the dialogue between us. Talk to me.

3

Your Husband and Man fo' Life,
Trae Macklin

*****

4

THE RESPONSE

By Tasha Macklin

Tasha

I was angry at Trae, so I refused to acknowledge his presence. He stood at the front door, on his way out. I walked right past him as if he wasn't even there.

"Why you got on my pajama shirt?" he asked me.

"Why do you care? You ain't here to wear it," I snapped and regretted the slip of my tongue. I kept walking, head held high until I got to my bedroom. My shoulders slumped and I sat on the edge of my bed, trying to fight back tears.

Trae had been playing these head games for the last two weeks and the shit was starting to get under my skin. We hadn't had sex in a while and my hormones were raging. This nigga would come home and spend time with the kids, and on those nights when he would stay, he slept in the guest room. In the morning, he'd fix breakfast and then leave. Some nights he would put the kids to bed and leave as if I was no longer in the picture. I'm like: What the fuck? Nigga, you made your point when you came and got my ass, so why you gotta drag the shit out?

For the last week or so he had been home every night. So

seeing that, I was like: Okay, this game is finally over. I thought since he wanted to communicate through letters, let's do it. Getting a letter from Trae was new territory for me. So I figured since he wrote a letter, so could I. I thought it over for a couple of days and then I sat down, grabbed my pen and paper and I wrote. I poured out my heart.

Dear Trae,

I can't start this letter with apologies because truthfully I am not sorry for the shit that I did. Regretful? Maybe. No, that's a lie. I am sorry some days, sorry that I fucked with you. I read your letter and I felt everything you said, and I took it all into careful consideration. The fact that you sat down and wrote a letter gave you points in my book, but the pain you caused behind your actions that caused you to write it, fucked that up.

I never wanted to see us get to a point where seeing each other hurts. I know that you love me; there is no doubt in my mind of that fact, but you said it best yourself, you fucked up. It was you who fucked the next bitch. It was you who allowed the streets into our home, only to invade and crumble the very foundation that we fought hard to establish. I can't love you for both of us, Trae. I gave you everything you asked for. I gave in to you against my better judgment and gave you all of me. I gave you three beautiful children. I gave up my career to be your wife and raise our children. Then I gave up my dignity when I had to walk into a doctor's office and have them look me in the face and ask how many sexual partners I had because I had a fucking STD.

It was me who sat up nights when you were in those streets, praying that you would make it home. It was me, who when pregnant, begged you to get out the game. And then when you had to make one more run, I had to bear the burden of losing our first child. Even when I didn't know if you were dead or alive, I never turned on you. I never left your side. In fact, I hauled my black ass to that jail when I found out you were okay and did the only thing a loyal bitch of my caliber could do: I stood by you through it all. And yes, I'm the same bitch that slept in a hospital chair for three months while pregnant again, nursing you, bathing you, and crying and praying for God to give you back to me. I refused to leave your side. Then to have you come back from death's door and years later pull the bullshit that you have been pulling. That shit is a slap in the face.

I'm tapped out, Trae. Not only have you fucked up, you put your hands on me. Love isn't supposed to hurt. Because of my love for you, I haven't loved me. I haven't been caring about myself enough to secure my feelings. Was fucking your boy's brother wrong? Hell yeah! I can't deny that. But knowing that I was giving you just a taste of what I went through was priceless. Was it payback? Shit . . . Payback ain't enough for what you put me through.

I wanted this letter to be a confirmation of my anger, but the more I write the more I realize that I still love you more than life itself. I can't throw away all of the good times that we had, all the drama we fought through to be together. I can't throw away the love that we share for each other. I can't forget the look in your eyes when you say the three words you love to hear and seem to know before I do, "Tasha, you're pregnant." Then the look on your face when you hold our baby in your arms for the very first time. And I damn sure can't forget that you are and have always been a provider and protector of our family. I too sat and thought back to how it all began with the chase, the catch, and the mind-blowing sex that kept a bitch cumming for hours. Yeah, I'm your butterfly, and yes, I whisper your name when you hold me close, because when I'm in your arms I lose my breath.

I don't want to hate you, Trae. What I wanted was for us to live a perfect life, but that shit obviously doesn't exist. We both fucked up and we fucked up bad, but going over the shit repeatedly does not change things. If we ever plan to get past this, there has to be some major changes.

I want to love you without pain again, Trae. I don't want to think the dick is all mine. I need to know it is. I need you to keep the streets away from our children and me. Keep them away from the home that we built together. And most of all, I need my Trae back, the Trae that doesn't lie to me. The Trae that doesn't hurt me. And definitely the Trae that would never put his hands on me. I know it wasn't easy on you when you found out I gave your pussy to another man, and it damn sure wasn't easy for me to know that the next bitch was getting my dick. But I think it's fair to call it even. If we can get past this, we have to bury this shit and start over fresh. No hate, no anger, no bringing the shit up when we feel down or get angry. We have to kill it.

First thing's first. Cali is a dead issue. This move fucked us up. We need to relocate. Second, we have to repair everything that is broken. Third, we have to love harder than we have ever loved before, having no secrets and holding no grudges. I love you, Trae. I want to be proud again to say I'm your wife. I want to be able to hold my head up high and not feel like the next bitch's joke. Lastly, I want my Trae back. The man that I first fell in love with. The man that had a bitch doing lap dances in the club. The Trae that had a bitch giving up pussy anytime and anyplace. The same Trae that holds my face and gives me tender kisses when I'm sleeping, and lays in bed with all of us around you and laughs at the crazy things our children say. I want my King back.

I don't want to live without you, but I know that we have a long road ahead of us before we can get back to life as we once knew it. If that letter was you opening the line of communication between us, I heard you loud and clear. And this is a sincere response. We need time to heal and whatever happens next has to happen on both of our terms.

Love Always,
Your Wife Tasha

*****

Three days went by and he hadn't even acknowledged that I wrote the damn thing.

But the kicker for me was, tonight I wanted some dick and this nigga was at the front door on his way out. *I could just kill him*, I thought to myself as I sat on the side of my bed and grabbed some tissue and blew my nose.

"What did you say smart?" Trae eased into the bedroom startling the shit out of me. I didn't even hear him come up the stairs. Now I grew even madder because he busted me crying. He stood in front of me. "What did you say smart?"

I rolled my eyes. "You heard what I said, Trae. You ain't here to wear the damn shirt."

Of course he had his signature smirk plastered on his face. The smirk that said, "Yeah, I won. I got the upper hand." The smirk that I wanted to smack clean off his face. He walked away, took off his jacket and threw it across the loveseat. He then leaned up against the dresser and stood there staring at me. "Fuck you, Trae!" I snatched up one of the pillows and threw it at him. I was mad, sniveling and blowing my nose. I felt vulnerable and more like a weak ass bitch.

"Take off my pajama shirt and come here, Tasha."

I ignored him. Tears were streaming non-stop down my cheeks, and I was still blowing my nose trying to get myself together.

"Baby, come here," he repeated.

This time I shook my head no. "Leave me alone, Trae. I'm not feeling you all up in my space right now." I was struggling, but slowly getting myself together. I stood and gathered my wet tissues. Fully composed, I looked back at my husband and said, "Make sure your ass is gone when I come out." I went into the bathroom, shut the door and then tossed the tissues into the trash. I placed a warm washcloth over my face until it cooled off. I slid the cloth onto my neck and looked at my red and swollen eyes in the mirror. Unhappy with my reflection, I turned the water off and hung up the cloth.

When I cracked the door open and peeked out, Trae was posted up in the same spot where I'd left him. I snatched the door all the way open and charged out. "Don't you have some place else to go?" I asked. When I got close enough, he pulled me close and hugged me.

"Trae, no. I see what you are doing." I tried to break free of his embrace. "You won. You got me back here. You got your family together and now you don't want me. And at the same time, you won't let nobody else have me. It took a minute, but I see right through your bullshit."

"That's not true."

"I'm not stupid. Get off of me and get the fuck out!" He held me tighter.

"Till death, Tasha. Till death do us part."

"No, Trae. I'm not going to let you do this to me."

"Do what?"

"Control me like this. Now let me go."

"Aiight, fine. You're in control," he said and let me go.

"Now leave," I told him as I pulled the covers back on the bed. I needed some quiet time without him all up in my space. I grabbed my Sudoku puzzle book and a pencil. Trae began to undress in front of me. Butt naked, he went into his jacket pocket, came out with a blunt and headed for the bathroom. I heard the shower come on and a few minutes later, the smell of purple haze floated up my nose.

Trae

Tasha obviously got my point. She was mine, always would be, and I would never, as long as I was breathing watch her run off happily into the sunset with the next muhfucka. Took her long enough, but I believe she got it. Yeah, I was doing all that shit on purpose. I had to bring that lesson home somehow. I intended to drag the shit out a few more nights, but when she came walking past me with my pajama top on, ass hanging out, my dick started hollering, "My nigga, did you see that?"

I started talking back. "Yeah, I saw it."

"Well, what the fuck you waitin' on? Don't make me starve again tonight. I can't take this bullshit much longer. So what you gonna do about it?" my dick asked me.

"The pussy ain't going nowhere. Be cool. You'll be all right for a few more days."

13

"Man, you got me fucked up. You ain't starving me another night. I need to be all up in that." And at that thought, my shit got rock hard. The next thing I know, I was climbing the stairs to my bedroom, following behind my dick.

I knocked off half of the blunt and took a nice, hot shower as I thought about how many ways I was gonna fuck Tasha. I knew my wife like I knew the back of my hand, and she'd been uptight as hell these past few days, needing to get dicked down. That's why she was doing all that damn crying. She was sexually frustrated.

I got out the shower, dried off, brushed my teeth and lotioned up. When I stepped out of the bathroom, she was sitting in the bed, puzzle book in her lap, tissue in hand, wiping away her tears. I pulled my side of the covers back, climbed into our bed and slid up next to her. I began unbuttoning my pajama top, the one that she had on, and she stopped me.

"No, Trae," she stated firmly.

"I want my pajama top," I told her as I went back to unbuttoning it.

"I'm not playing with you, Trae."

"I ain't playing, neither." I snatched it open, popping off the last of the buttons. They went flying across the bed. Tasha rolled her eyes. Her succulent looking breasts left me in a trance. Before I leaned in to her, I put a tit in my hand, brought it to my mouth and sucked on her pretty brown nipple.

"Trae, stop!" she said through sniffles.

I didn't stop until I had enough and was sure that her pussy was wet. I snatched the covers off her, ran my hand up her thigh until I had two fingers inside her. Yeah, she was ready. I leaned back in and flicked my tongue across her nipple as I fingered her pussy.

"Can I get that kiss you been saving for me?" She shook her head no and moved my hand from between her thighs. I pulled her down toward me by the neck. "I want my kiss." Roughly, I covered her mouth with mine, kissing her until her lips kissed me back.

Just as Tasha began thrusting her hips forward and whispering my name, we heard, "Mommy, I want some water." Caliph interrupted as he stood in the doorway.

"Okay baby." Tasha broke away and tried to get up, but I stopped her.

"Caliph, drink some water out of that bottle right there on mommy's table and get back in the bed." I held onto Tasha's waist so she couldn't move. She still treated that boy as if he was a baby. I had to talk to her about that.

Caliph drank some water and set the bottle down. "Good night, Daddy. Good night, Mommy," he said as he made his exit.

"Close the door, Caliph." I still had work to put in.

I lay on my back, grabbed my dick and started rubbing him. He was so hard that when I turned him loose, he jerked back and forth all by himself. We both knew what that meant. "What you want to do with him? You want to tame him or what?" Tasha looked at him, trying to fight it, but just like my dick was talking to me, I knew her pussy was speaking to her.

She climbed over me, pussy in my face and her mouth at my dick. "Oh it's like that?" I asked her. I knew it was about to be on when I felt her lips wrap around my tool. Then, the next thing I knew my shit was down her throat. I couldn't let her outdo me, so I spread her pussy lips and ate her at the same rhythm as she was sucking my dick. Electricity shot down to my toes. It was obvious that my head game was winning; she released my dick and was moaning, groaning and grinding against my mouth. I could tell she was about to cum, so I slapped her on the ass and stopped.

As she changed her position, I grabbed another pillow and put it under my head. It was time to watch my baby ride. She locked gazes with me as she straddled my dick and slid all the way down on him. She whispered, "Trae, I hate you right now, but this dick feels so good." Tasha placed her soft hands on my chest and started ridin'. I watched my baby get her fuck on, sliding up and down, side to side until she finally screeched, "Oh my God! My spot. My spot!" I gripped her ass and plunged into her pussy as deep as I could. "Oh that's my . . . right there, baby. My spot. Oh my God, that feels so good."

I got a kick out of seeing her face twisted all up and could feel her pussy contracting. Once her head fell back, I knew she was gone and she started cumming. My shit throbbed and was now on maximum swole. She fell forward on top of me, and I whispered in her ear, "I still want my kiss." Tasha was still breathing hard and trying to recover from that orgasm. Still deep inside her, I turned her onto her back and placed her legs over my shoulders.

"Baby wait," she purred.

"Wait for what? I'm the nigga you love to hate, remember?" I was on my knees digging deep. She couldn't move; she couldn't get away. All Tasha could do was roll her head from side to side and moan. I had complete control of the pussy.

"Trae, baby, please. Ohmygod! Baby, my spot. My fuckin' spot!" she screeched, and at the same time she started cumming again. It was on. In this position, there was no hittin' and missin'. All I could do was hit it.

"This is what you needed, right?" I asked her as I kept punishing her spot.

"Okay, baby. I had enough." She shuddered all over.

"But I didn't come yet," I teased her. "You don't want big daddy to cum? That ain't fair. I know you said you hate me, but damn." I was so deep into the pussy, that when I did decide to cum she was getting pregnant. Her body trembled as I got my grind on nice and slow. I lived for these moments.

"How does this feel?" I asked her. She was so gone, she couldn't even answer. I guess my baby had, had enough. "I need you to come one more time for daddy." I rocked her body in sync with mine. Her pussy was feeling so good, I knew I wouldn't be able to hold back much longer. The pussy at this point . . . was bliss. "C'mon baby, move with me. You can take this big dick a little bit longer." Finally, my baby rolled her hips for me. We were as one. Fucking at the same pace. Slowly. Those slow orgasms seemed to be a little more intense than when you were fucking wild and hard. The slow ones came up on you from deep within. Finally, we started cumming at the same time.

Tasha

I hadn't realized that I needed some dick that damn bad. I went from having a crying fit and on the verge of telling him to go fuck himself, to, I really love sucking your big black dick and I love you more than life itself. Love is crazy I tell you. Looks like I'll never understand the shit.

Here we lay at the foot of the bed and I couldn't even remember how we got here. I believed I came at least three times. Lying on my side with my eyes closed, Trae gently kissed my shoulder and told me how much he loved me . . . And my pussy. I knew he was sincere.

That was the last thing I remembered as I woke up to my phone ringing.

Angel

"I need a damn vacation," I mumbled when I heard a series of knocks on my office door.

"What!" I yelled out, annoyed because I had just decided

to take a break for at least an hour. Things had been a circus around our office for the last few days.

My door flew open. "Good morning, Mrs. Santos. You are not going to believe this." I could hear the excitement in my assistant's Deidra's voice.

"Believe what, Deidra?"

"You have got to see this," she said, coming around my desk and placing her Nook in front of me. Why she was reading on her Nook smack dab in the middle of the workday, I had no clue.

"What are you doing?" I tried to move back.

"I can't tell you. I have to show you. First, look at this." She tapped my keyboard and began typing. Twitter appeared on my screen and then I saw a page that read: *Trae Macklin.* I sat there waiting to see what this shit was all about. She scrolled down the page showing me bits and pieces of conversations about Trae publishing *THE LETTER.* It appeared that he had been chatting with random females about his and Tasha's relationship. I had a chance to read a few tweets, and then she held up her Nook revealing a book cover. The title was *THE LETTER* by Trae Macklin, and there he was posing on the fucking cover with his damn chest out. I was like: What the fuck is this?

As I read this 'apology letter,' I tried to hold my composure in front of my secretary, but inside I was losing it. "Okay, thank you," I said in a tone that let her know she was dismissed. She smirked and took her little Nook from me and slowly began exiting my office. She was one of them bitches who had a thing for Trae.

"I'm on break so hold all of my calls," I told her.

The second that door shut, my fingers were on speed dial. "This bitch better answer."

Tasha

I looked over at the clock, then at my ringing phone. I started not to answer because I could feel that it was getting ready to be some bullshit. Against my better judgment, I took the call.

"Why you always call me so early?" I asked, still half asleep.

"Bitch please, its noon over here and I need to talk to you," Angel yelled.

"What's up, Angel?" I asked, already knowing that this was going to be a daunting conversation.

"Why did that little secretary of mine just walk into my office and show me your husband's bullshit Twitter page?"

I took a deep breath. I was not ready to have this conversation, so I hoped to push it off until I had a chance to wake up and prepare for the onslaught of questions coming my way. "Can we talk about this later?"

"Heeeell no, Tasha," she responded, not backing down.

"It's not that serious, Angel."

"He's on Twitter and on Nook. God knows where else. What is going on? He's telling all of y'alls business."

20

"Trae wrote me an apology letter. I read it and then threw it in the garbage. He found it and got pissed off, and then posted it for his little fan club on the Internet."

"So that's how we doing it now? Posting shit on the Internet?" Angel asked with an intense sarcasm.

"For real, I don't know what Trae is into nowadays."

"Bitch, that is your husband. You should know everything that he is into. Posting your shit online. . . ."

Angel obviously was feeling some type of way over all of this. Wait until she found out I was getting ready to post my shit as well. She'd probably have a heart attack.

Angel

I sat on the other end of that line trying to read her emotions but couldn't. Tasha was always good at hiding shit.

"So what are you and Trae doing over there? Because I saw your little post on the end. And don't tell me that you are even thinking about doing the same bullshit!"

Tasha took a deep breath then answered, "We are trying to get things back on track.

"Angel, I never would have thought that we would end up this fucked up."

I could hear the pain and despair in her voice. But I would have to feel sorry for her later because I had a few things I needed to get off my chest.

21

"So, are you going to post all of your business, too?"

"No, Angel. I'm not."

"Good. Because I can't say it enough. Y'all moved way out to fairytale land and lost y'all gotdamn minds. And while I'm on the subject, that snake ass cousin of yours, no disrespect to the dead, but he saw that shit coming. Him and Trina had major roles to play in all of this bullshit. Trae's ass went and jumped into some foreign pussy and then you turn right around and fuck family."

"Look, don't judge me." Tasha was getting all riled up. "He started the shit and I finished it. He knew what type of bitch I was when he married me. I told him up front, 'Fuck up and I'ma have some serious payback for that ass.' And I meant that shit. I don't know why y'all can't seem to understand that."

"I don't have a problem with payback. He fucked up, no doubt. But out of all the dicks in the world, you had to slide on Kyrons. Tasha, you are not that naïve. You had to know that it would cause a major riff between Trae and Kaylin."

"Honestly, at the time I didn't give a fuck. I was doin' me. Shit, I'm grown. I can fuck who ever I want."

"Doin' you? Don't hand me that bullshit. Ain't no *doin' you* when we are a family. And now your shit is in jeopardy because you were so-called *doin' you*." A couple seconds of quiet passed. "Tasha, you are my girl and I love you to death, but Kaylin is my husband. His whole brotherhood with Trae has been compromised."

"If your husband is going to let what happened between

me and Trae get between them then they need to reevaluate their so-called brotherhood," Tasha stated.

Silence fell over the line. I couldn't believe what she had just said. "So you really don't know what Trae did to Kyron?" *Fuck me!* I wasn't supposed to say that. Loose lips sink ships. This was exactly why Kaylin didn't want me talking to Tasha. He knew I would be the one to spill the beans.

Tasha

I sat straight up in the bed, put my feet on the floor and braced myself for what Angel was about to reveal.

"What happened, Angel?" I asked.

"Oh, don't ask me shit. Ask Mr. Internet."

"Don't play with me." I stood up and walked to the window to see if Trae's truck was outside, but it was gone.

"Hold on, I have another call." Angel obviously thought she was going to dodge my question.

"Angel, don't you fuckin' answer that call. What happened?"

"I gotta go."

"Angel, wait! You bitch!"

She hung up.

SHIT JUST GOT REAL

By Tasha Macklin

Tasha

I couldn't believe Angel hung up on me after not telling me what Trae did to Kyron. I called her ass back and of course, she didn't answer. *Why was I so out of the loop? And what did Trae do to him?* Shit, he was laid up in a hospital bed the last I heard.

I dialed Trina. Now that I thought about it, it had been weeks since I'd spoken to her. When she didn't pick up, I sent her a text and then I called Trae.

"Hey babe, what's up?"

"You tell me. You do remember our conversation, don't you, Trae? We had an agreement. No more secrets, no more lies." His silence let me know that he could sense where I was going with this. "I heard some shit about what you did to Kyron, but I want to hear it from you. What did you do to him, Trae?"

"We'll talk when I see you."

"*We'll talk when I see you?* What is that supposed to mean? Just tell me what you did to him. How hard is that?"

"Why the fuck do you care, Tasha?" he barked. I then knew that I had to choose my words carefully. "Tell me. Why the fuck do you care?"

"Forget it, Trae." I took a deep breath, regretting where this conversation was headed.

"Forget it my ass! You called me asking about the next nigga. And when I tell you we'll talk about it later, you start pressing me. What the fuck is that about!"

"Forget it, Trae." I hung up on him. Frustrated, I folded my arms, sat back in the chair and began running Angel's words through my mind. Fearing the worst, I picked up the phone and called Trina again.

"Hello."

My sister sounded as if she didn't mean to answer the phone. "I just tried to call you," I told her. "What's up with you? Where have you been? I haven't heard from you."

"Trying to stay my ass outta trouble. What's up with you?" she answered, all dry and shit.

"Trying to find out what's going on. What's happening?"

"Shit," she said all nonchalant.

"When is the last time you spoke to Kendrick?" I didn't have time to beat around the bush.

"Last night. Why?"

"So what's up with Kyron?"

"What do you mean 'what's up with Kyron'?"

25

"Trina, don't play dumb. Trae did something to Kyron and I know you know all about it."

"I don't know shit, Tasha. If I did, you know I would have told you."

I thought about what she said, though I wasn't totally convinced she was telling the truth. "If I find out you lying it's going to be on and poppin'."

"Do you think Kendrick would tell me something if they did do something to him? C'mon now, Tasha."

Okay. Now I know this bitch is lying. She probably don't believe the words coming out of her own damn mouth. Something isn't right. I just can't put my finger on it...

"Yeah, all right Trina. Let me get off this phone. I'll talk to you later." I hung up and jumped out of bed. Then I threw on some jeans and a T-shirt, brushed my teeth and washed my face. I went downstairs and thought about how convenient it was to have Aunt Marva around. The kids were finishing up breakfast. I kissed my sons and Aisha on the cheek.

"Marva, I gotta go check on my sister. Can you keep an eye on them until I get back?"

"As long as you're back by two. Me and Cheryl are going by Daisy's."

"No problem. I will be sure to be back by then."

"Ma, can I go?" Shaheem asked me.

"You are not even dressed, Sha. Mommy gotta go and check on Auntie Trina. I'll be right back."

During my drive to Trina's, I kept thinking about Trae asking me 'why do you care'. Shit. *Why was I so concerned?* I knew damned well why. I couldn't front. I did catch some feelings for Kyron. It was mostly lust, but the feelings were there. I hated to admit it, but it was fun while it lasted and it felt damned good to give Trae a dose of his own medicine. Of course, I didn't love Kyron, and Trae had my heart. I knew Kyron and I could never be. Trae would never allow that to happen, and on the real, neither would I. More important, I will always be in love with Trae Macklin.

I arrived in front of Trina's place in thirty minutes flat, shut my ride off and headed up her stairs. I knocked on the door and waited. As I stood there, my mind flashed back to that day when Trae stood out here pacing like a raging caged animal waiting to pounce. Quickly, I tossed that scene out of my head. I never want to go through that shit again. Again, I banged on the door and then pressed my ear up against it. I knew the bitch was home because her car was parked out front. I pulled out my key and used it.

"Kendrick, is that you? That was quick. You came back?" Trina came from the back wearing a wife beater, shorts and sweat socks. I saw a dark purple bruise on her arm and when I looked closer a bruise was healing on her jaw.

"What the fuck happened to you?" I squinted as a frown came over my face and I eased into investigation mode.

"He dumped me, Tasha." Tears started rolling down her face. She folded her arms over her chest and looked down, avoiding eye contact. "Kendrick dumped me. Can you believe that bullshit? The nigga dumped me!"

So that's why I hadn't heard from her ass. I followed her into the kitchen. She filled up a teapot with water.

"You want some tea?"

"Tea?" I asked her.

"I got cramps, bitch. Yes, tea. You want some tea or not?"

"No, I don't want no gotdamn tea. What I want to know is what happened to your fucking face?" I walked over and grabbed her chin, turning her toward me.

"What happened, Trina? How did you get the bruises? You let the nigga beat on you?"

"Hell no! Me and his bitch got into it." She pulled away from my grip.

"He got a girl?" I grabbed one of the kitchen chairs and sat down. She didn't answer my question. Instead, she decided to get right to what I wanted to hear.

"After Trae stabbed Kyron in the throat, all types of skeletons started falling out the closet. They thought he was going to die, girl. After that happened, the nigga flipped the script. That's when the nigga started treating me like I was the enemy. I was like shit, I wasn't the enemy when Kyron was fucking my sister and I was fucking you!" She grabbed a cup and a tea bag.

"Stabbed him in the throat? Damn, you brushed past that shit like you were asking me if I wanted paper or plastic.

How long ago did he stab him, Trina?"

"It's been almost a month."

"A month? Why are you just telling me this?"

"I don't know." She shrugged. "You got enough shit to worry about. Plus, you told me to stay out of your fucking business, remember?"

No the fuck she didn't, I thought, looking at her sideways.

"And why do you care anyway? I thought he was just a revenge fuck? Let me find out you done caught feelings for this nigga," she said with a half a smile as she began pouring hot water into her cup. I wanted to toss that shit in her face.

"You know what, Trina? Fuck you. You told me what I wanted to know. Let me get up outta here." I stood up.

"What? I hit a nerve?" the bitch had the audacity to ask me.

"No, you didn't. I'm good." I threw the same fake ass smile back at her.

"Then why you got to leave when I mentioned that you caught feelings?" She sat down and crossed her legs.

"I gotta get up outta here, Trina. But I'ma tell you this, there is one thing for sure and two things for certain: Karma is a bitch." I walked out, leaving my miserable sister all by herself. I didn't know her involvement in the shit, but something was up.

As I drove back home, my thoughts were on Trae, and the reality of his actions felt like a mack truck smashing me into brick wall . . . *He almost killed the nigga. How was he able to get that close to Kyron to stab him in the throat? And how did I not know about this? What if he would have killed him? Now what? Are they going to keep going tit for tat? This shit has to stop somewhere.*

"How are you, Mrs. Macklin?" I heard the greeting come from my opposite side as I pulled into my driveway.

"I'm okay, John," I said to the mailman. Instead of putting the mail in the box, he handed it to me.

"Have a good one," he sang, and then started whistling.

"You too." I parked the truck in front of the garage and went into the house. I set the mail on the dining room table.

"Marva, I'm back," I yelled as I tossed my keys onto the table. On my way to the kitchen, something told me to look through the stack of letters. I picked the stack back up. *Junk. Junk. Bill. Junk. Bill. Junk.* I tossed each one on the coffee table. Then I came to a red envelope addressed to me. It had nothing for the return address, but the postmark was from New York. I started to tear that shit up, but as I flipped it over, that unmistakable fragrance struck my nose. At that moment, I knew where this shit came from. *Speak of the devil.* My heart pounded double time at the thought of what could be inside. I dropped it on the table and stared at it. Folding my hands together, I brought them to my mouth as I contemplated whether I should burn the shit or open it. Just as I had decided to burn it, curiosity got the best me, causing me to snatch up the envelope and find a corner somewhere.

"Marva, I'll be upstairs!" I hollered, and then I heard

little people running my way. "What I tell y'all about running through the house?" My three sons stopped dead in their tracks.

"Send them out back. I'll be out there," Marva yelled out.

"I'll take them outside, Auntie Tasha," Aisha said.

I stood there and watched my wanna-be-grown niece line the boys up and give them instructions as she pointed her little finger at them. Then she marched them out of the dining room. I headed upstairs to my bedroom and shut the door. I went over to my desk, sat down and slowly opened the letter. If felt as if time stood still. I began to read . . .

Tasha, Tasha, Tasha . . .

There's a part of me that wants to knock you the fuck out, then stomp the shit out of you while you're on the ground. But another part of me wants to give you a hot sponge bath, pat your body dry with the best towel money can buy, then plant kisses all over your body before I make love to you all night long. This Love-Hate thing may sound crazy but I'm not insane. I didn't just smoke some dust before I penned this letter, and I ain't poppin' pills like some white boy from a trailer park in Milwaukee.

I'm pointing fingers and you're the target. You led me to think you was divorcing that muthafuckin' clown Trae. You fucked me, allowed my seed to start developing in your womb, made me think I was the shit times ten, then after I done went against my own brother for you, at war with your punk ass husband over you, and what you do? Go running back to this lame nigga Trae and tell me I was just a revenge fuck. Then to top your bullshit off, you get on some right to choose Planned Parenthood shit and abort my child. Our Child. Fuck abort, you killed our child. On some G shit, you ain't no better than me and every other thug that caught bodies on the street. And as vexed as I am, as unbelievable as your actions are, a part of me still got love for you.

The funny part is, this whole shit revolves around you, but it ain't about you. It's about Me. This shit may sound insane, but I ain't crazy. See, you are one of them high-maintenance Hos and the problem with high-maintenance Hos like you is y'all think your pussy is made of platinum and your clit is a 10-carat princess cut diamond. I don't know about Trae and all these other tender dick clowns with they nose up your ass like it's a bouquet of roses, but every move I made with you was calculated for my benefit.

You're probably saying to yourself right now, "You wasn't talking all that shit when you had your face between my legs or when I was riding your dick!" The typical response from a Ho who don't understand men. You riding my dick is about Me. Me bustin' a nut, Me laying back while you work, Me proving that your high-maintenance ass ain't no different than these broke Hos in the projects fucking for Chinese food and a Tyler Perry flick. Me, Tasha. It was always about Me. Bottom line.

Although it may not seem like it, the same shit goes for me eatin' the shit out your pussy. The better I eat your pussy the better you gonna ride my dick. Nine times out of ten you

32

Hos go running back to your friends bragging, then your friends come creeping behind your back into my bedroom. So even when it looks like I'm going all out to please you, I'm doing some minor shit to benefit Me in a major way. Half you Hos never had an orgasm anyway, so all it takes is for me to give you one for you to return the favor and unconsciously convince your friends to fuck me by bragging to them. Angel, Kyra, Jaz.

You think none of them ain't entertain the thought of creeping into my bed like crackheads wasting they time chasing that first hit? Go figure.

You probably thinking I'm full of shit because I'm the same dude that copped you a brand new Jag. If you thinking like that, you must've really went for that bullshit about me not being able to have you running around the city flagging down taxis. Then you went bragging to Trina about the car being in your name. Only if you knew it was in your name because it was a stolen car that was tagged. And as far as you riding around town, yeah I wanted you in something hot. The better you look, the richer I get.

See, motherfuckas in the hood is nosey, always got some shit to say and they always countin' somebody else's money. And everybody run with the winning team. Reebok ain't come to some underground rapper for a sneaker deal, and Bill Gates ain't give no dude with a 99-cent ebook a million dollars to promote it. Reebok went to Jay-Z for them S.dots and Bill Gates pieced off Jay-Z with a mil to promote Decoded. Money attracts money. If people think you got money, they think you know how to make it. So they'll put their money in your hands. You know how many people gave me bricks on consignment because of you? How many people offered me buildings to set up spots because they see you in that Jag? Every time your silly ass zipped up and down the street in that $90,000 car that only cost me five stacks, you caused some up-and-coming hustler to get at me so they can find out how to get behind the wheel of a car that do 0-60 in less than five seconds. I got two goons in Brooklyn that will kill for me and a top lieutenant off the strength of your pretty ass whipping that Jag. How could I not love you? But you were just as happy as a Ho on payday to be in a car you think is increasing your wealth while all you were doing was raising my stock. Good lookin'. I appreciate that. Even though the spotlight was on you . . . it was always about Me, Tasha. Never forget that.

When I say I love you, I'm really saying I love Me. That may sound crazy, but I'm not insane. There really is no you; Tasha just don't exist. Your Jag, I bought it. I picked the model, the color, all for a specific reason that really had nothing to do with you. But your stupid ass started to define yourself by that car. Same thing with the money I would give you to tear down the mall with. And you had your weight up already, your own money. But I wanted you to splurge with mine. So the car you drove, the clothes you wore, even the perfume on your skin, all of that was an extension of Me.

Why do you think I was so caring and nursed you back to health after you twisted your ankle running from Trae? It seemed like I cared about you, but I cared about you being *able to hit the gas on that Jag, hop out and walk around switching that big ass, keeping men thirsty and people talking, wondering about how much money I got. All because I could toss it around on you. Why do you think men call women Hos? It ain't got nothing to do with you fucking, at least for me anyway. Everybody like fucking. It's about you hittin' the pavement and strollin' your ass around town, so you can make me look good and attract potential investors for me. You're nothing more than a walking billboard.*

Remember, Tasha . . . I may sound crazy, but I'm not insane. So when I say I hate you and love you–don't take it personal. It really has nothing to do with you. It's all about Me.

Dueces
Kyron, that boss ass nigga

*****

I ran through the pages in minutes and by the time I got to the last page I was fuming.

"No this muthafucka didn't." I sat there stunned. I started not to even dignify that bullshit ass letter with a response, but fuck that! He obviously felt he needed to get some shit off his chest, well so did I. I opened the drawer, grabbed my favorite notepad and a pen and started writing this bitch ass nigga back.

Just as I finished and was about to read it over to make sure I didn't leave anything out, Aisha came barging into my room yelling, "Auntie Tasha! Kareem bust his head. He's bleeding. Aunt Marva said come here. You might have to take him to get stitches." She was sweating and all out of breath.

"What?" I jumped up and hauled ass downstairs to check on my son.

Trae

Right before I got some bullshit ass phone call from Tasha, I was actually on my way to talk to her. Not *talk* to her, more like tell her some things that I had been keeping to myself. I was going to tell her what went down with that stalking, crazy bitch Sabirah and what I did to Kyron, especially since the shit was most likely caught on camera. If the detectives or really care or if Mama Santos or someone decided to press the issue, I'm fucked. Benny, my attorney, said my biggest concern was my prints. If my prints popped up, that would change the whole fucking game. The worst of this shit stemmed from Sabirah, and if I get picked up, Tasha needed to be prepared. Then to really rain on my parade, I get a bullshit ass phone call from Charli. This ho calls me out of the blue talking about she needs to see me. So I definitely needed to get to Tasha and tell her this shit before I made my next move; then here she comes calling me, drillin' me on some 'what I did to the next nigga' bullshit. I pulled the phone back and looked at it, thinking she obviously was smoking something.

When I got to the house I walked up in there ready to go to war.

"There you are. Where have you been, boy? And why don't you live here anymore?" My aunt met me at the door with her nosey ass. I paused and looked at her like she was crazy, but she kept on going. "Anyway, Tasha left to take Kareem to the hospital. He fell on that pile of bricks that you have back there and he's going to need stitches. Take that frown off your face. The boy is not dying. He will be fine," she said it all casual as she began picking up toys off the floor.

"Fine my ass. Who was supposed to be watching them?"

"Boy, they are kids. Kids play. They run, they get hurt. So watch your mouth. We can't watch them 24-7. Shit happens," my aunt snapped.

"Who's here now?" I looked around her.

"Tasha took Kareem and Aisha with her to the hospital.

Caliph and Shaheem are having lunch. Are you hungry?"

"Naw, I'm good."

"Good, because I gotta get out of here. Daisy and Cheryl are waiting on me. Glad you came home."

"Do I have time to jump in the shower right quick?"

Aunt Marva looked at her watch. "Boy, you better be glad I love you. Hurry up!"

We were just on the court shooting some hoops and I was sweaty as hell. I hit the stairs and at the same time started taking off my T-shirt, looking forward to a nice hot shower. Better yet, I wanted to jump in the pool and do a few laps.

When I got to my room I walked straight to the closet, tossed my tee into the hamper and grabbed my trunks. As soon as I walked out of the closet, I saw that Tasha had been at her desk. Her little flowery notepad was flipped open and her fancy pen lay on top of it. *Awww shit.* We hadn't been spending time together, so I was hoping she didn't write me no Dear John letter. I went to the desk and my eyes went to the sentence, "and don't write me no more, bitch!"

What the fuck? Don't tell me Charli is up to her bullshit again, sending letters and shit. I flipped to the front page and saw *Kyron, Kyron, Kyron.* I was hoping that my eyes were playing tricks on me. I focused and those three words were still there. I thought I was about to lose it. *Why the fuck is she writing this lame? And in my house. No wonder she wanted to know what I did to this faggot. This bitch done lost her damn mind. She still fuckin' with this nigga?* I couldn't even see straight, let alone sit down. I ripped the pages out of the notebook and forced myself to read this shit.

Kyron, Kyron, Kyron . . .

First of all, Nigga, you bitch made. Here it is you over there recovering from a life threatening injury and the first bitch you holla at is me? You talking all that shit about Jags and money and connections, who the fuck you tryna convince that you the shit, me or yourself? Talking about you love me and you hate me. What kinda fag shit is that? You wish you hated me. You don't know who you fucking with, so you better check my resume. I will bet anything that your dick is hard right now as you read and anticipate my next line.

My nigga, why can't you just accept it? You were just something to do for me . . . simply a revenge fuck. I gave you some payback pussy on my terms and you got pussy whipped and fell in love. That's why you laying over there crying and shit. And you have the audacity to call me a Ho? Fuck outta here with that bullshit. You don't even know how you mustered up the energy to call me a Ho. No nigga, I ain't your Ho; you're my bitch. Sheeeit . . . gonna call me a walking billboard? If I am that, you best believe it reads, "Kyron's a fuckin' sucka!"

I recall you saying three important things: 1. You went out 2. You made my money 3. You kept me fly, then gave me the dick if and when I decided I wanted it. But then I fucked you so good you thought I was going to take you to the top of the world and had you begging: Marry me, Tasha! Be mine, Tasha! I had your punk ass pulling out rings and shit. So, that sounds like you the Ho. Nigga, I pimped your ass real good, had you trained well, and even after you got that ass whipped you still brought momma her money. Yeah, I rode your dick . . . good enough to make you lick where another nigga slides his dick. How does Trae's cum taste? Is it as good to you as it is to me? And then you brag about a bitch serving her purpose. No nigga, you served your purpose. I wasn't even fucking you and you were coming up off stacks and scheming on ways to steal me from Trae. And you are boasting about a Jag? You a low budget ass nigga if you think a Jag gets you a come up. Them fake ass, so-called, loyal niggas you got on your team are laughing in your face because they got a bitch for a boss, or should I say a broke ass co-worker? Bitch ass sitting here whining about a car, page after page. Nigga please! I bought Trae a fuckin' Maybach. And you obviously forgot that I told you I have a Spyker C8 Aileron Spyder sitting in the garage that I don't even drive! That Jag was like a punch buggy compared to my shit. That's why Trae busted the shit up. You think your money is long? Get the fuck outta here; your money is as long as your dick . . . and that ain't long enough.

Since we keeping score, let me Ho check your ass real quick. You called me a Ho, but I'm the same bitch that had you turn your back on your family. It was Me, Tasha, the same bitch that had you eating pussy, and it ain't about you making me cum, nigga, I'm married to Trae Macklin. My pussy is well trained. And yes, I'm the same bitch that turned you into a marked fucking man. So watch your back, bitch ass nigga. You do the math. Calculate that shit. Tasha, a ten... Kyron, a zero.

You asked yourself, are you insane? Hell no! You in love and I can't fault a nigga for that. You just like every other nigga that gets the pleasure of Tasha. You sprung the fuck out. The proof is in that long ass letter going on and on and on about what you lost and what you wish you still had. Gonna write me a punk ass letter. I can't get over this shit. What? You ain't got shit else to do? By the way, where your bitch at? You had a so-called bad bitch that held you down the whole time you was doing your bid, but as soon as you fell into this boss pussy you forgot all about that bitch. I had your ass moaning and groaning my name. Tasha. While thinking Mari who?

Oh, and I didn't kill your seed. The little muthafucka committed suicide when it realized it wasn't the child of a real boss. So fuck you and die muthafucka!

The Boss Bitch,
Tasha Macklin Forever
P.S. Don't contact me no more. Bitch!

I finished that shit, not knowing what to think. I stood with the shit in my hand as my blood began to surge through my body like hot lava. *She caught feelings for this nigga?*

"What are you doing reading my shit, Trae?" I didn't even hear Tasha come in the room.

It was on . . .

*****

Fifty Shades of Trae

By Charli Li

In my diary and on these pages, I write from the very heart, sharing my most intimate feelings. These pages are my calm in the middle of the storm that I call Trae. Up until now, I've never found the need or urge to record my most private thoughts or sentiments.

There is no greater pleasure than the firm, yet gentle caress from another woman's man. The heat from my lips tainted with desire and deception. Hungry strokes filling every aching crevice. Lying awake craving a forbidden love. I've come to realize that the only one who can truly understand the strength of a powerful man is a powerful woman.

Who am I? The daughter of Jamaican woman named Lucinda, who passed away when I was almost seventeen. My father, Charles Li, is a full-blooded Chinese. Their journey is a set of diary pages all in itself. But these entries are about me. They specifically chronicle a volatile time in their daughter's life, my life. Charli Li, a bad bitch and a very powerful woman from the top of my head to the tip of my toes, through the blood coursing through my veins. Nothing I crave has ever been denied. Married men, single men, I don't have a preference, because I am irresistible to every man. My only desire, however, is for one.

Am I bragging? Allow me to reintroduce myself. I am Charli Li, a twenty-eight-year old, only child and heiress to the Li throne. Or shall I say Li and Li Holdings, Ltd. Commercial real estate and land acquisition, buying and selling businesses are our specialty. We are also major players in the banking industry.

As a real estate attorney, I am also the face of the Li Organization. Nothing comes through the organization without my eyes and ears being privy to it.

So when Stephon Macklin, an associate of mine, who often sends business my way, called in a favor, I was happy to oblige. He told me that his cousin, Tasha, who was a newlywed and expecting her first child, was relocating to the Los Angeles area. She and her husband needed a house. In fact, they wanted a big house and money was not an option. That caused my ears to perk up. He also mentioned that Tasha's husband having some money to invest.

And that's how it all began . . .

January 10th

Today was almost business as usual, meaning, instead of meeting with our high profile multi-million dollar clients, I was preparing to meet this street thug, Trae Macklin. When Stephon first told me that he wanted to introduce us, I thought, What for? It would probably end up being a waste of my time, and what could he possibly bring to the table? My table? And invest? At most he probably had a suitcase filled with a million dollars in crumpled bills. I was also certain that he didn't have the prestige that would qualify him to do business with me. So, I immediately came to the conclusion that he would be a waste of my valuable time, and I performed a due diligence check, anticipating the worse so that I could tell Stephon I wouldn't be able to take a meeting. But to my astonishment, I discovered that Trae Macklin needed to unload a cable company he had acquired, that he had no interest in running. He also had some funds he needed to wash. But when I dug a little deeper, I was surprised to learn he had more than a few dollars to play with. Stephon obviously had been holding out on me. However, I still needed a face-to-face and to hear his exact agenda in order to make a decision to do business with him.

I sat at my huge, mahogany and glass, Donald Trump-styled desk wondering if I was going to have to dismiss my undeserving prospect. My intentions were to keep our meeting as brief as possible. But as soon as I laid eyes on him, my tummy did a nose dive. I quickly looked him over, analyzing his every move and gesture, desperately searching for a flaw . . . any imperfection. Needless to say I couldn't find one. His teeth were perfect and sparkling white. Nails were apparently manicured, even and clean. His clothes tailored his body just right, and his incredibly smooth skin brought to mind a piece of dark, rich, sweet chocolate.

To my surprise, he was very articulate. For some reason, I was expecting loud and boisterous, choppy English, and half-sentences. I, Charli Li became mesmerized as he gave his spiel, putting his offer on the table. He had meticulously calculated how his money was going to work for him and just how I was going to be instrumental in making that happen. Evidently, Stephon had told him a little too much about me.

As I told Mr. Macklin about a new land deal he should consider, I struggled to maintain eye contact. The intensity of his stare sent chills through my entire body. His lips were moving, but all I could do was focus on how I wanted this man.

Without a doubt, he definitely won my stamp of approval. It was safe to say he didn't carry himself as your average 'Negro from the hood' as often portrayed in the theater, and this intrigued me to the point that I was fascinated by this rare find. Hours after our meeting was over, I was still caught up in thinking about him. For the moment, Trae Macklin, a brotha captured my attention and that didn't happen very often.

January 12th

Behind closed doors, business and pleasure becomes one and the same. Playful flirting is just an undertone for a possible late night get-together, but I have no time for games. A woman of a lesser caliber might have to take her time, but when I see something I want, I'll go get it, even if I have to take it by force. What's the point of window shopping if you can afford the whole damn store? With Trae Macklin, I'll admit, my curiosity got the best of me. I've spent the last few nights fantasizing about his touch, visualizing his hands squeezing my buttocks and his tongue licking my thighs, finding its way up to my love button. I'm a Daddy's girl forever, but a good girl I never was, and Mr. Macklin had me wanting to be very bad. It's not like me to be thrown completely off guard by this schoolgirl crush I've recently developed over him. Who was I trying to fool? I don't just need him, I want him! And I always get what I want.

January 15th

Sunday Night at Club New York

Tonight I incidentally made the acquaintance Mr. Macklin's wife. I stopped by his club after hearing Stephon speak so highly of it. Plus, I was instrumental in putting the deal together, so I figured it was time for me to witness the fruits of my labor.

I guess it was a "date" night because there she was, all snuggled up under him as he periodically whispered in her ear. I looked her over. She's all right, but she wasn't Charli Li, heiress of the Li Empire. They eventually got up, and at first, I just stood in the background, watching as they moved on the dance floor. Then I found myself fantasizing that those same muscular arms were caressing me. Damn! I could only imagine the precision of his stroke, and how good it would feel to have his strong but gentle hands brushing all over my body. At that point, I decided to do a little something to see if I could rattle the wife's cage. He led her to the elevator—the perfect spot and opportunity to make my move. I slithered over to where he stood pressed up against her ass, wishing it were me.

"Excuse me. Mr. Macklin, may I have a moment with you?"

I surprised them both. She turned toward me, looked me up and down.

"Charli, this is my wife, Tasha," he said. "Tasha, this is Charli." He kissed her cheek. I knew the game very well. I was getting under his skin. "Charli, what's up?" He questioned me.

"I have a proposal that I think may interest you."

"Make sure you give it to Benny."

Mrs. Insecure pressed the elevator button, obviously letting me know the conversation was over. She then turned and tongue-kissed him, but that didn't deter me.

"I came here to talk to you, since I have been unable to

reach Benny." I then set my gaze on Tasha. "Can you go get us something to drink?" I asked her.

"Do I look like the help to you?" she spoke sharply.

"Charli, I'll have Benny call your office tomorrow."

"Don't have him call. Just come by." I glared at Tasha as I gently and boldly placed my hand on his bicep and flashed my sexiest smile at her. I then turned and walked away, enjoying the steam I could feel coming up off her head. All I did was make my presence known, and just like an obedient puppy, she barked and jumped. But Mr. Macklin, on the other hand, responded when our eyes met. I could feel the heat that existed between us. He tried to maintain a strong façade, but it was apparent to me. And his bitch, Mrs. Insecure, she felt it too. Her reaction confirmed that she could be easily ruffled. So, I made up my mind to send Mr. Macklin a little gift. And I knew just the thing to send. My goal was to get her out of the way—one way or the other.

January 20th

Hood rat bitches are so predictable. You can dress them bitches up and give them the finer things in life, but the fact remains, they are still rats. Just as I planned, his bitch didn't like the gift. She called my office threatening to have the $50,000 custom-made Harley Davidson stripped and sold to a junkyard. I laughed because she wasn't doing anything to me. I wiped my ass with 50 grand. If it were me, I would have simply sold the bike and went shopping.

After she hung up, I anticipated Mr. Macklin's call. Sure enough, it came a little over an hour later. When his voice bellowed in my ear, full of aggravation I knew I had succeeded.

"Yo, what's up with you? Why are you sending shit to my house?"

"Ooh, straight to the point," I purred as I spun in my chair. "I heard that you were thinking about a Harley, so I had one brought over. No big deal. It was just a simple gift."

"Don't send shit to my house."

"Was it the color?"

"Yo." He laughed, seemingly caught by surprise at my question. "No, it wasn't the color," he mocked.

"Mr. Macklin, I can get whatever color you like? Just say it and it's done."

"Charli, listen to me. You don't have to buy me shit! And definitely don't be sending shit to my house. I'm telling you that for your own good."

"So, I see. It's the wife. Maybe I'll stop by with someone and have them pick it up. Maybe I won't. However, I'm not to be denied, so I suggest that you handle her." I hung up the phone.

The average woman would have been fazed by the apparent anger he displayed, but all it did was add fuel to my already raging fire. Tension in the Macklin house is just what I needed so I could make my next move. Thanks to you, Mrs. Macklin, your insecurities just pushed your "husband" that much closer to my bed.

January 24th

Today when the man who wouldn't leave my mind walked into my office, I had to call on all the gods to keep me from jumping on him. Damn! He is soooo sexy. The intensity of his stare and the deepness of his voice had my pussy wet. I was forced to cross my legs to control the throbbing between them. I reached out to collect some paperwork, and when his fingers slid across mine, I got a tickle in my stomach. Oh my god! This man has me consumed, mind, body, and soul. I can't wait to feel all of that power deep inside of me.

January 30th

Today was a blessing in disguise. I stopped by Club New York and marched upstairs to his office. When I knocked, Stephon opened the door. I know I shocked everyone as I stood there looking picture perfect, wearing an all-white Chanel dress and white stilettos. Stephon gave me a hug, and Marvin stood up and gently shook my hand. Mr. Macklin obnoxiously kept his back to me.

"Mr. Macklin, I'm glad you're here. I have some documents for you to look over. I'm telling you, you and Stephon are going to love this one. How about a resort in

Barbados?"

He swiveled the chair around so he could face me. "I told you to take all business through Benny."

"Benny has been damn near impossible to reach. So here I am."

He stood up. "Yo, Marvin and Steph. Let me holla at this girl in private."

"Not a problem," Marvin said and was the first to stand up and leave.

I had put together the perfect proposal for a resort that Mr. Macklin and Stephon could add to their real estate portfolios. I addressed Stephon as I handed him the folder, "This is for you." He took it and left out, closing the door behind him. Now I was overjoyed that I was going to be able to steal a few private minutes alone with Mr. Macklin. I knew I had to seize the moment.

"Check this out, shorty. You official on the business tip. And I'm feelin' your swag. But it ain't nothing personal between us. I told you several times to go through Benny. But you don't seem to get it. So what's really up? What do you want from me?"

"What do you think I want?" I know what came over me. I sure did, because I couldn't control myself as I took hold of his manhood and got on my knees.

"Whoa!" He grabbed my wrist. "I don't think you want to do that."

"Yes, I do and you can't tell me that you are not the least

bit curious." I massaged what I wanted right out of his sweat pants. To my enjoyment, it immediately stood at attention. I ran my tongue hungrily over the tip, tasting that sweet, dark chocolate, and when some liquid oozed out, I knew I was in control.

"Yo, you know this is going to cost you, right? And way more than some fuckin' motorcycle. By the way, wifey sent that shit to the junkyard."

"Anything you want. Just name it." My tongue was already exploring all nine and some inches. I was loving every lick.

He kept looking at the monitors. "Yo." He grabbed my head. "Get up." As I looked up into the slits of his eyes, I then took him to the back of my throat. I couldn't leave without giving him something to remember me by. Reluctantly, I eased him out of my mouth.

"Get up." He repeated.

I stood up and began to unzip my dress. I wasn't done with him just yet.

"You know you got me fucked up. My wife is downstairs, so I hope you got your shit off because you gots to go," he said as he stuffed that massive hard-on back into his sweats.

"What? Is she coming?" I was completely turned on at the thought.

"That ain't the point. I said you gots to go."

I was fine with that because I had succeeded at getting

what I wanted, and it was just the beginning. Being the powerful woman that I am, I couldn't let him get away with all of that dick. I was convinced. That was just way too much good dick for one man to possess.

"Well, I do need to get going. I am running late. Make sure you and Benny go over that file. You'll see that the offer is very generous." I grabbed my briefcase and left. Now I could move to phase two of my plan.

Instead of leaving as he instructed, I went downstairs and stood in the back of the room. He had made it downstairs and joined his wife, who was seated at one of the VIP tables. I watched their interaction. Mrs. Macklin was giving him the cold shoulder. Knowing I played a huge part in stirring up her anger felt intoxicating. There I was, strategically planting the seeds of mistrust and division in their relationship. Satisfied that I had seen enough, I boldly sashayed over to where they were seated. Three other young ladies accompanied them. I leaned over and whispered in his ear, "There is plenty more where that came from. I'll do whatever you want me to."

I heard her friends yelling obscenities, but I kept on walking. I wanted to get a rise out of the insecure wifey, but this time she didn't bite. Being that close to him once again, caused me to lose control. I was supposed to leave, but I couldn't. At that exact moment, I felt like a lioness, carefully stalking her prey. He had me. I ended up paying the bouncer a generous fee to situate me right back upstairs in Mr. Macklin's office.

As I watched the security monitors, I knew I succeeded in my endeavor. Once Mrs. Macklin abruptly stood up, he grabbed her wrist and yanked her back down. The bouncer, whom I paid, came over and whispered something to Mr. Macklin. She used the opportunity to jump up, snatch away from him, and her girls were right behind her as they disappeared out of the club. Come to mama!

Meanwhile, I watched as he sat and listened to who I believe was a comic on the stage. My Mr. Wonderful never cracked a smile. He was driving me insane. Finally, he got up, and within seconds, he was entering his office. I didn't know what to expect. He walked over to me, and I was dying to savor his tongue, but he turned away and placed the tenderest kiss I had ever felt on my neck, sending my hormones into overdrive. As he positioned my petite frame on his desk, I braced myself to feel him. His hands strongly caressed my body as I watched his manhood rise. Anxiously I sat as his hands moved skillfully up my thighs causing my skin to heat up.

When he pushed his fingers inside my silken walls, my heart dropped to my womb. It was happening. I closed my eyes and lay back, while spreading my legs wide, welcoming him. He plunged himself inside the wetness of my tightness and began to stroke. I thought I would pass out. How could a dick be this good? I was floating, and gripped the edge of the desk as he filled every inch of me. His attention was divided between the ringing phone and the monitors, but it didn't stop him from hitting my spot and riding it until I came long and hard. I was in love, and dazed by that powerful orgasm. As he slid out, I admired my sticky juices on his long, black shaft.

"You gotta go. I gotta handle something."

I stood up. "Mr. Macklin, I need to handle something as well." While he answered a call, I went to my knees and swallowed his thick length until I felt it hit the back of my throat. After a few seconds of wet tongue and tight jaws, he released, hot and slippery, into my mouth. And yes, I drank every drop. As he looked down at me with glassy, yet satisfied eyes, it was confirmation that I had won. His dick was now calling out my name.

February 1st

I had to admit that was the best dick I had ever tasted and fucked in my twenty- eight years on this earth. I couldn't stop thinking about the escapade. My kitty wouldn't stop tingling. I recognized the challenge involved in making him mine, so I decided it was time to raise the stakes a notch. What's the use of having money and power if you can't manipulate the world so that everything is yours for the taking? My father always says, "The only way to predict the future is to have the power to shape it."

February 14th

Today is Valentine's Day, and I called Mr. Macklin with intentions on interrupting whatever he and his wife had going on. Tasha answered the phone with an attitude.

"Is Mr. Macklin available?"

From the dead silence, it was obvious she was stunned by my boldness.

"Who is this?"

"Charli. Charli Li, his attorney. Is this Mrs. Macklin?"

She didn't answer, but I could hear them speaking in the background.

"Sit down and take this call, Trae."

"Who is it, baby? Damn, it's Valentine's Day. When can I go pick up my car?"

"That's what I'm saying. It's Valentine's Day, and at this rate I may cancel that fuckin' car."

"Are the kids okay? What are you talking about? Cancelling? Why you trippin'?"

"The kids are fine."

"What up?" Mr. Macklin finally spoke into the receiver.

As I prolonged my conversation, speaking of things that could have waited until tomorrow, I sensed the tension in his voice.

"Give Benny a call." Was all he said before he hung up.

If I couldn't enjoy him on this day, I would at least enjoy the pain it caused wifey every time I contacted him. Hell, after all, it was Valentine's Day, and I chose to be alone. A first for me. She may well have him in her presence, but with his every touch, you better believe I will be in the back

57

of her mind.

Again, mission accomplished. Another nail in the coffin.

February 22nd

Damn near two weeks later, and I didn't have the opportunity to get another taste of that sweet dick. I was losing patience and half-doing my job at the office. I couldn't stop thinking about him, so I decided to pay him a visit. Since he hadn't come by to pick up the latest documents I had for him, I decided to drop them off at his home.

I rang the bell and waited patiently.

Mrs. Macklin snatched the front door open. "Can I help you?" She gritted her teeth, placing her hand on her hip.

"Is Mr. Macklin in? I only need to drop off these files." I pointed to the boxes on the ground. "Do you mind picking those up and taking them inside?"

She looked down at the boxes and then back at me. "Oh, that won't be a problem. Give me a sec," she said and left me along with the boxes standing there. She then reappeared and held the door open, inviting me in.

"Thank you." I was genuinely surprised by her kindness. "I know we got off to a bumpy start, but I'm not all that bad. Maybe we can do lunch sometime," I told her.

Mrs. Macklin closed the door behind me, and her mood turned dark in an instant. She was up in my face damn near kissing me. "I'm going to tell you this one last time. Stop calling my husband, stop buying him gifts, and don't bring your ass by the club, and especially not on this property ever again. Do you understand what I just said?" She uttered with a fancy roll of the neck.

"Excuse me? Mr. Macklin and I have business together. And this house? I'm the one who made it possible for you to live here. And the club? I arranged the financing on that. The club wouldn't even be in existence without my help. So if you think it's any more than just business, you need to have a frank discussion with your husband." I rolled my neck the same way she did.

Then the bitch had the nerve to sock me in the mouth. She grabbed my head, damn near twisting my neck off and kneed me in the face. I only got to punch her in the mouth when Mr. Macklin burst through the front door. He picked her up, swooping her into the air. A total stranger came in the door, damn near knocking me down and grabbed me.

"Get your hands off of me! Do you know who I am? Trae, who is this? Tell him to get his hands off of me!" I yelled out in disgust. I didn't know this man.

"I'm Detective Bryant, if you must know."

"Rick, get her ass out of my house, please," Trae said.

"Yeah, get that ho out of here before I put my foot so far up her ass, she won't be able to breathe!" Mrs. Macklin screamed.

The stranger took me outside and waited until I got into my car and pulled off. He didn't even bother to ask if I was all right. The wife may have won this round, but I'll be damned if she wins the next one.

March 9th

Since our little incident at his home, which I quickly got over, I heard through my sources that he was not staying there. Apparently, she put him out, and he was living in a condo about twenty minutes away. I had to see him. My body ached for him, craved his touch and attention. Once I got out of the luxury vehicle, I looked around, slammed the door, and made my way up the walkway and onto the porch. I rang the bell, and as soon as he saw me, his huge smile turned into a frown.

"Hello to you, too," I said as I pulled the screen door open and waltzed right in.

"Charli, what are you doing here? It's one in the morning." He slammed the door shut.

I took off my shawl and laid it on the couch. "Why else would I be here at one in the morning? It was all fine and dandy when I was on my knees, swallowing you to the point of no return—was it not? It's always business with you. I make you millions, and you can't even show me a little bit of appreciation?"

"What?"

"I want to be shown a little bit of appreciation." I meant exactly what I said.

"Oh, I'm supposed to fuck you, just because?" Trae came toward me in one fluid motion. "You don't know who you are fuckin' with, do you?" He wrapped one hand around my neck.

I gasped. My heart began to race as I anticipated what he was going to do next. He then began tugging at my dress. When he got it above my waist, he pushed me over the chair. "This is what you want, right? You want to be appreciated, right? What? Daddy's little girl wants to feel appreciated?" His manhood was pressed against at my opening. I was so thrilled that I wasn't wearing my Vickies.

"Not so fast," I moaned. But he was already plunging inside me, and it hurt. Slowly, I relaxed, and his rhythm began to feel good to me. "Yes, like that." I encouraged him as I fucked him back, contracting my pussy muscles trying to gain control. I could feel him growing harder, once again taking me to heaven. I wanted this moment to last forever, but I felt my orgasm coming on. My body trembled, and my legs shook as I crashed over the edge screaming out his name. He slowly pulled out of me.

"Fuckin' bitch!" he mumbled.

"Why are you so angry?" I asked him as I tried to get myself together. I was so in love with this man.

"What difference does it make? You got some dick, right? That's what you came here for, isn't it? What else do you want?" He went to the front door and opened it.

For the tiniest moment, I stood in awe. I couldn't believe he was treating me like a two dollar whore. Unnerved, yet satisfied, I fixed my dress, and said, "I can't believe you. Your club is going to be raided and—" I paused to allow that little bit of information to sink in. Ready to make my exit, I grabbed my clutch, pulled out a check for $270,000, and shoved it in his hand. He looked it over. "Before you say anything, I know it's short. But give me some time."

"Short is an understatement. Bitch, we talking eight million!" He looked as if he was foaming at the mouth. "Charli, don't fuck around with my money."

"Calm down. You aren't the only one who came up short with this last deal. We all did."

"Charli, eight million?" You got me fucked up. I suggest you get on the phone and talk to your father, or see whoever it is you gotta see and get me my fuckin' money. I ain't fuck you and put my most important shit at risk for a measly $270,000!"

"Give me a few days, Mr. Macklin." I waltzed out with my head held high. After all, I won this round.

Nobody, and I mean nobody, had ever treated me that way. I was so aroused that I went outside to my limo and played with my pussy all the way home. Mr. Macklin had driven me to enter new territory.

April 16th

I know it has been a while since my last entry, but I have been terribly sick. I ate a bowl of fresh kumquats. I knew they were full of acid, but they were so delicious. On top of the vomiting, I broke out in hives. I must have had an allergic reaction to them, and promised myself I would never look at one again, let alone eat them. Now I am too sick to even think about leaving my house.

April 22nd

Today I finally made it to the doctor's office. Yes, I did have an allergic reaction to the kumquats. However, that was the least of my worries. I must have sat in my car for an hour staring out of the window. I was in shock. Why? Because after previously having hundreds of tests, I was told that I couldn't bear children. My uterus was supposedly out of position. And coupled with that, I am usually pretty good with using protection. I let my guard down completely with Mr. Macklin. I couldn't believe it. One blood test later. Me? With child? What am I going to do? There I sat, pregnant by a married man. What will my father say?

May 1st

I had mixed emotions when I thought about whether to inform Mr. Macklin that I was pregnant. Something about him makes me feel like I'm more of a woman, but those mixed emotions were still there. At first, I toyed with the thought of not telling him I was pregnant. But eventually, I decided it was only fair to let him know. So I called him and gave him the good news. His reaction was one I never expected. He laughed and hung up the phone. In a rage, I immediately sent over a courier to hand-deliver him a copy of the pregnancy test.

May 2nd

Shortly before noon, my cell rang. I knew he would be calling me about the test results that were delivered.

"You thought that I was playing some sort of cruel joke, Mr. Macklin?"

"How did you let this happen?" he asked me.

"How did I let this happen?" I asked, utterly appalled. "You attacked me, or have you forgotten?"

"I suggest you get an abortion. Fuck that! What the fuck am I saying? How do you even know it's mine?"

At that question, I exploded. And then he exploded. The conversation ended with him threatening me. I told him that I was leaving for Seoul, North Korea on business for a while, and I needed some time to think and to decide on my next move.

May 30th

I am so sick today. I can't even pick my head up off the pillow. The weird part is, in all of my discomfort, I am still the most joyful woman in the world. I have actually made it to eleven weeks. I can only pray my baby will arrive safe and healthy.

June 19th

Today has to be the happiest day of my life. I had my first ultra sound and I even heard the heartbeat. I became overwhelmed with emotion at the thought of another life growing inside me. I'm sitting up in my bed as I write, rubbing my belly. I, Charli Li, who was told that she would never bear children, am carrying Trae Macklin's baby. This is so unreal.

I have been in Seoul for almost two months now, and I am ready to head back to the States.

August 3rd

While I was gone, I was able to keep up with Mr. Macklin's affairs through Stephon. Therefore, I knew just how to strike upon my return. I also had someone tailing periodically. I knew the majority of his moves and whereabouts.

From the airport, I went straight home, showered and changed. Then I headed straight to his condo. After being away for almost three months, to say I was anxious to see him was an understatement. What kind of welcome would I receive? I wondered.

For almost two hours, I sat parked across the street from his condo before he showed up. Excitement throbbed in my tummy as I walked up on him as he opened the door. He said, "Charli, what the fuck? Do I have to buy one of the Rosetta Stone CDs and learn to speak your language? Because every time I tell you in English to leave me the fuck alone, you act like you don't understand me. What could you possibly want at three in the damn morning? Wait. Let me guess. You've now become a stalker."

"Don't flatter yourself. I didn't come here to bicker with you."

"Then what the fuck did you come here for?"

I looked up into the handsome face of the ebony god who stood in front of me and struggled to maintain my composure. I tried to read his eyes, but they were void of any emotion. "I came for three reasons. To tell, to give, and to show. Now, if you would be so kind as to let me in, I can say and do what I came here to do and be on my way."

I watched him run his hand across his face and then his beard stubble. Exasperated, he said, "And for some reason, this couldn't wait until a reasonable hour? You just had to come here at three in the morning?"

"In China, they say the early bird catches the worm."

"What the fuck? You a philosopher now? They say that shit everywhere. Look. I'm tired, Charli, and I'm ready to blow. The only thing you can do for me is give me the money you owe me from the investment on that land project. I don't want to hear about no fucking birds and worms."

"I got what you want. But I am not going to conduct business out here on your front steps. Now, may I please come in?"

"You got five minutes and five minutes only." He opened the door and waved me inside. I closed it behind me.

"I know I'm probably the last person that you want to see right now," I said as I followed him to the living room.

"No shit?"

I ignored his sarcasm . . . for now. "We definitely need to talk."

"You're now down to four minutes. Just give me what's mine."

I reached into my Louis Vuitton shoulder bag, withdrew an envelope, and handed it to him. He tore open the envelope with the check in it. I filled him in on several business matters that he had an interest in.

"This check concludes our business. Now, I need you to stay away from me and my club," he replied over his shoulder as he pulled out one of those blunt things. He lit it and sat on the couch, inhaled twice and began to cough.

"Put that out, Mr. Macklin," I said facetiously and walked a few steps toward him. "I'm pregnant, and second-hand smoke is bad for my child. Our child."

"This is my house. And I suggest you stay your ass over there then. Why are you coming closer to the smoke? As a matter of fact, why are you still here? Because I ain't tryna hear that 'our baby' shit right now."

"Hear it now or hear it later, Mr. Macklin." I pulled the Tyvek envelope out of my bag and tossed it in his lap.

"That's a sonogram that I had recently. I wanted you to see what you created inside of me."

"Charli, don't you think I already saw the first one you sent me?"

"I don't know. You don't return my calls, so it's obvious that you don't care. But if you want to continue to deny my child, our child, that's on you. The baby will be raised to have the best of everything, and I will not force you to be a father. I have enough love inside of me for the both of us."

"Are you done? Because I'm starting to feel like I'm trapped in a Lifetime movie. I'm not in the mood for this, Charli. I just told you that." Trae inhaled the blunt thing again. "You said you came here to tell, to give, and to show. You told me about the baby, which I already knew. You told me what you did for my club, which I want you stay away from. You gave me the check, and you showed me the sonogram . . . again. Your time is up."

Since I knew all of the drama he was experiencing with his wife cheating on him, I was patient. Stephon graciously filled me in. It was evident that he felt defeated by everything going on in his life, and I couldn't help but take advantage of the situation. "The sonogram was a part of what I came to give. I have something else that I want to show you." I moved so I could stand directly in front of him.

"And what might that be?"

Stepping out of my Alexander McQueen's, I lifted my skirt and pulled my thong panties off.

"Charli—"

Leaning forward, I put my finger to his lips. "Don't talk. Since this is the last time that I might see you, just lie back and let me show you something that I learned in the Philippines." Lifting my skirt to my waist, I straddled my ebony god, slow winding my body. His dick grew exponentially in his pants. I was soaking wet. "They call this the 'Couch Canoodle'." I reached under me until I felt his zipper. In seconds, I had his member free, big and thick in my hand. I rose and rubbed the head of his dick all around my wetness. Quickly tiring of the foreplay, I lowered myself a few inches onto him. "Earlier you said I had five minutes. How many do I have now?"

Before he could say a word, I leaned forward to kiss him. He turned away, but I didn't care. I was getting what I came for. Using my pussy muscles, I pulled him all the way inside me. He didn't even budge. I bounced up and down on his dick until my pussy adjusted to his length and girth. Then with my legs splayed apart, I bent my knees and pressed them up against his chest, and then slowly leaned all the way back until my palms were flat on the floor. Pregnant or not, I was almost completely upside down. Without letting his dick escape from within me, I thrust my hips back and forth while opening and closing my legs simultaneously. And just when I thought he might not take the bait, he grabbed me by my hips and began to match every stroke. I was confident that by the time I started working my pussy muscles like the Kama Sutra had taught me, I would have Trae Macklin exactly where I wanted him. I put some pussy on him that had him moaning and holding me tight. I believe he mumbled something about pregnant pussy being his weakness.

You know a strategic and manipulative bitch like me was going to capitalize on that. My mouth watered with every stroke. This man was more than just smart and sexy. He was powerful, and I felt every inch of his power as his dick touched what felt like my soul. Check mate.

Tears formed in my eyes as I began to cum, and a painful reality followed my joy with a reminder that he would pull out of me and go back to her.

August 8th

My father sent for me today. He wants to send me to Thailand to handle some business. His timing couldn't be more perfect. Since I refuse to abort my child, Mr. Macklin is so upset with me. I get the impression that he wants to kill me. As my father was giving me my instructions, he looked down at my belly and I quickly turned away. I am nearly five months and can barely hide it. If he knew I was pregnant, there would be hell to pay. I am indeed dancing with danger.

I have a lot of thinking to do, but mostly I must figure out how to justify my actions to my father.

August 14th

Angry that Mr. Macklin wouldn't take my calls and refused to see me, I pulled the baby card, and I sent Mrs.

Macklin a picture of the sonogram and signed it, yours truly, Charli Li.

August 26th

Mr. Macklin sent a message to me through Stephon to meet him at the club. I knew he wouldn't be able to stay away, and I understood that he was under a lot of pressure, thanks to me. Immediately, I started planning on what I was going to wear, how I was going to smell, and what gift I was going to buy him. I'll let you know what happens. Oh yeah, the baby has been constantly fluttering. My heart smiles every time it happens.

September 8th

I can't believe it's all over. What I thought would be another opportunity to bask in the essence of Mr. Macklin, was all a trick. When I walked up the stairs, expecting to see his pearly white smile, instead, I was greeted by a dark heart. Mrs. Macklin stood, questioning and threatening me as if I were a child. Of course, I remained calm, refusing to allow a bitch of her pedigree to faze me. I quickly realized it was a set up and decided to leave. Before I could get a firm handle on the rail, the evil, scornful bitch tripped me. I fell down a flight of stairs, lost consciousness, and suffered a miscarriage.

Here I am lying in a hospital bed in pain, more mental than physical. The nurses are constantly coming in and out. I ask the doctor again, "Is my baby gone?" and he tells me the same thing, "Yes." My heart won't let me receive it. I cried so much last night I thought I would pass out. I can't believe Stephon set me up for that bitch to attack me and to destroy what I was told that I would never have. He obviously doesn't know that one of the creeds of the Li Organization is "A life for a life."

September 11th

When I awoke, I looked around and realized that I was in a room at my father's palatial estate in Rancho Santé Fe, California. I lay there, staring at the panoramic view of the clear blue sky. My whole body ached, and I noticed that I was attached to a single I.V. drip. The door to my room opened, and in walked my father with Luther, his best friend and my bodyguard.

"My child, you had me worried." He bent down and kissed my forehead. "At the hospital, before I had you moved, I was told you were with child, but you miscarried. I'm disappointed, Charli! You never told me that you were pregnant."

My father wasted no time in laying down the iron fist. One death deserved another. He mentioned killing Stephon, Tasha, and when he mentioned Trae, I lost it. I begged and pleaded with him to let me handle them all.

My father then walked over to my bodyguard, Luther, who was standing by the door. I knew what was going to happen as I turned away. Luther was my father's confidant, and was granted no mercy.

September 16th

I'm back at home left alone with my thoughts. I haven't left the house in almost a week. My father was so disappointed in me. However, I think he was more upset that he himself missed the signs. But what he didn't know was that I would have done whatever it took to get to Mr. Macklin when I thought that it was he who requested that I meet him at the club.

In my head I kept hearing my father's voice asking, "How did you let this happen?" He went into a tirade for almost an hour. I felt like a five year old all over again. I have to fix this. The worst part of it all is the love of my life doesn't want me and didn't want our baby. How did I allow myself to fall in love with a man I didn't have? I refuse to say 'a man I will never have' because I will make him love me if it's the last thing I do.

September 20th

Today was such a surprise. I was in the house I had purchased for myself when I needed to be alone and away from the world. But being in this big empty house was only making matters worse. I am feeling so empty. When my father left for an out of town business trip, I ran here. But not before sending a message to Mr. Macklin telling him where I was going. With every step across the cold marble tile, I was reminded that I had just been robbed of the greatest feeling in the world. The feeling of life. I made myself a cup of hot tea and sat down on my huge comfy couch. I was focused on recovering, when my bell rang. I got up, slipped into my silk robe, and opened the front door. There he stood. Mr. Macklin, looking as sexy as ever. He held a teddy bear in one hand and a small gift bag in the other. I let him in and closed the door. I was in shock. I couldn't speak.

When I turned, he gave me a big hug and whispered in my ear that he was sorry that all of this happened to me.

"Are you really? If so, then how could you hate me so much? Why didn't you want our child?"

"It's not complicated, Charli. I'm married. My heart belongs to Tasha, and it will always belong to her. It only becomes complicated when I fuck with you on a physical level. We were only supposed to get money together. That's it that's all."

I was crushed. "Then why are you here?"

"I only wanted to check on you and say that I'm sorry."

I couldn't control myself. I collapsed into his arms and cried on his shoulder as he held me tight. At that moment, all my disappointment and insecurities disappeared. He sat me down and handed me the teddy bear and the gift bag. I squeezed the bear tight and could smell his cologne all over it. In the bag was a small box.

When I opened it, my heart rate soared. It was the most

beautiful jade and diamond bracelet with a little dove hanging from it that I had ever seen. Once again, I knew this was the man for me. A man who pays attention. The first time I met him, I wore my grandmother's necklace with a small dove dangling from it. I couldn't stop the tears from falling. When we sat back on the couch, I pulled my feet up close to me and laid my head on his chest. I stared at the bracelet as it shimmered on my arm and contentment filled my heart. Trae held me until I fell asleep. When I awoke, he was gone, but the comfort and compassion he gave me would last forever. Today I love him even more. I don't care how complicated things are.

September 24th

I have been wracking my brain all day, trying to figure out how to keep Mr. Macklin in my good graces. I want so badly for my dad to meet with him and allow him into our fold. I am just going to have to stir some things up. My first order of business is to send Mrs. Macklin to a funeral, Stephon's funeral. He betrayed my trust. Then, one by one, they will all pay until Mr. Macklin is all mine.

September 27th

I've been instrumental in assisting Mr. Macklin with earning millions of dollars. One would think that I could get him to dance like a puppet on a string. But he does not. He's even more distant. I can't get any time with him. But I won't stop until he is doing exactly what I want him to do.

September 30th

It took a while, but I finally got my father to agree to meet with the love of my life. It was like trying to extract teeth from a shark's mouth. But because I am my father's only child, and he hates to see me in pain, he folded. If everything goes as planned, I will have Mr. Macklin right where I want him—that is, intertwined inside my web. I must admit, being rich, evil, and powerful is a terrible mix, but Charli always gets what Charli wants. I sort of feel sorry for Mrs. Macklin. She shouldn't have to be in turmoil because she is married to the man of my dreams.

October 17th

Today my father had a huge affair and invited Mr. Macklin so he could meet a few of the organization's members. This was a test, and he handled himself very well. I watched as he commanded the room. I was so turned on, seeing him sitting with my father talking business and his future with our family. I felt like a master. There was no turning back. My father told him the only way out of this family is death. I had him right where I needed him.

October 20th

Today I saw the love of my life kill a man. It was his first real trial. He carried it out without asking any questions. The only way to be truly trusted in this family is to have blood on your hands. Unquestionable blood. There he stood, death in his eyes and a gun in hand. Heat coursed through my veins as I watched his victim lie merciless at his feet. Most women would be turned off by the sight of blood and brain matter painting the floor. But for me, it was the total opposite. My lover has a beast in him that I craved to be next to. I tingled as I watched him walk away as if it were nothing. I need to be under him, to feel that force up close and personal. And I am scheming on making that happen within the next couple of days.

October 25th

This morning when I rolled over to see the empty space, my body ached for just one more touch. He had been gone for hours, but his body heat still rose above my sheets. What is it about this man that renders me incapable of control? My body and soul yearns for the power of his presence, and at the same time it's shattered by the reality that he belongs to someone else.

Heavy is the heart that carries the burden of many lies. I lay wondering, does she really know what she has? I hated the very thought of her. Is hatred too strong of a word, or does it shield me from the true emotions of "the other woman" that I have become? I have to face it. I am alone, waiting in the shadows of their love, ready to pounce on every opportunity to have just a small piece of him. Trae

Macklin, will you ever know what your touch does to my existence?

As I collect the sheets from my bed and inhale deeply, the scent of his cologne remains a memory of our passion that had just set my room on fire. Am I in love? No, I'm obsessed.

October 29th

Today Mr. Macklin was all about business, barely making eye contact with me. He was cold, disconnected, and not trying to hide it. I was very much hoping that I would get an opportunity to go to my knees and take him deep inside my mouth. But no such chance. Whatever was going on outside of what we shared had his mind, heart, and spirit consumed. I guess—no—I know it has something to do with that bitch; she is enough to drain the life right out of any man. I don't understand why he stays with her, subjecting himself to so much anguish. Especially when I am offering him a way out.

November 10th

Today while on the phone with a very important client, Trae walked into my office holding a bouquet of black roses. He didn't say a word. Instead, he stood there smiling at me. My heart began to melt instantly. Why does he take me on this rollercoaster ride? I grabbed the roses, touched them against my nose, and then laid them down. I was about to wrap up my call when he came around my desk, placed me on top, and stood between my legs. I tried to get him to wait, but before I knew it he was inside me and stroking slow.

My attention was torn between business and pleasure. I put the caller on hold and allowed him to have all of me. As he exited the office, he sealed the deal with a single wink. I spent the rest of the afternoon on fire. God, I love that man.

Signed,

Charli Macklin . . . Oohh, that goes well together!

But then it hit me . . . black roses?

November 14th

Today Mr. Macklin and I were back at square one. I think he loves to piss me off. We sat at dinner, going back and forth about taking on more work for the organization. I saw major things developing for him within the organization. He surprisingly told me to stay out of his dealings with my father, that it was none of my business.

"What? Stay out? Have you forgotten that I run this business?"

"But you don't run me, Charli. Remember that. I run you."

I wanted to take that wine bottle and crack it up against his damn head. I looked over at him, then down at my plate and became sick to my stomach. Who the fuck does he think he is? I am definitely not the bitch that he went home to every night. I got up from the table, grabbed my clutch and left. I heard him call me, but I didn't even turn around. Fuck him!

November 22nd

Trae is an asshole, excellent lover, amazing person, family man, cold-blooded killer, fearless, crazy, calm, calculating, stubborn . . . I could go on and on. There are undoubtedly, Fifty Shades of Trae, and I am well aware of over half of them. But it is official. I'm done. It is going to be business only from this point on.

November 25th

Today I'm in a really bad place. I know I said that I was done, but it's been over a week, and I have not seen or heard from him. I feel like shit. Last night, for the first time, I cried. Without him I feel so empty. I wanted to call his phone but couldn't. Being torn between love and hate is torturous. How can a man make you feel so good, and then at the same time cause you so much pain? I think I need a vacation. I'm in love and confused.

December 1st

Today, Mr. Macklin paid me a visit. When he walked in the door I didn't say a word. I walked to my bedroom, showered, and then crawled between my bedding and proceeded to go to sleep. When I felt his warm breath against the back of my neck, I assumed he was here to make peace. I felt as if I had won. He turned me over and got on top. I thought I would lose my breath. His lips and tongue moved slowly across my breast. When his hand slid firmly up my inner thigh, I arched my back as his fingers tickled that spot deep inside me. As he grabbed my leg in his arm and began to ease in, I braced myself for all his length and thickness. Breathing heavy and holding him tight, I begged, "Fuck me." And he did just that.

By the time he was done, I swear I couldn't remember my name. Damn, I love that man. And guess what? The next morning he got up and made me breakfast. I had no idea he could cook. I walked into my kitchen to see him standing there wrapped in a towel and fixing two plates. I didn't know what I wanted to put my mouth on first, him or the food. More to come.

December 3rd

I was devastated. I saw the love of my life and his other half together. There they were inside the toy store in the mall with the boys laughing and playing. My stomach knotted up as I thought about the child I lost. I covered my mouth in an effort to hold back the tears, but I was afforded no such luck. I turned and walked into a store and went straight for the dressing room, sat down, and cried. A gut wrenching cry. Regardless of what happened between me and Mr. Macklin, she had no right to kill my child. The only comfort I have was in knowing that what goes around comes around.

December 5th

Today was a hell of a day. Ever since my dad started these new business ventures, I have been in and out of the country. Physically and emotionally, I felt drained. I was so tired I didn't even want to think about him. I just wanted to take a hot bath and crawl under the bed.

When I opened the door to my house, I was surprised to see a trail of yellow and pink roses leading to my living room. As I followed the trail, I became more and more excited with each and every step. I had forgotten that I slipped him a key to my place. There he sat with a sexy smile and devious look in his eyes. I placed my briefcase on the coffee table and took a seat next to him. He poured me a glass of wine and signaled me to place my feet in his lap. After removing my shoes, he began to massage my heels. Once his hands started to wander up my thigh, my day changed from bad to good. He slowly removed my panties and went to his knees. This would be the first time he tasted me, and I have to admit his tongue game is deadly. I squirmed to be free, but he had me locked in his grip, giving me one mind-blowing orgasm after the other. I never came like that in my life. Once he was satisfied with his work, he picked me up and carried me to the bathroom, undressed me, and put me in the tub. He kissed me on my forehead and left me to relax. I put my head back, thinking, I'm such a lucky bitch. As I crawled in bed and grabbed my diary, all I could say was, "God, please keep him safe. Just the thought of not having him in my life pains me something awful."

December 10th

The love of my life and I leave for New York tomorrow. We have a sit down with one of the heads of the Chinese families. I'm hoping that we have time to get naughty after the meeting. My fingers are crossed. Details when I return.

December 13th

Well, business wise, the trip was a success. But at some point, he ran across the wife and I ended up coming home alone. What type of hold does she have on him? Why is it so hard for him to let her go? I will tell you this; if he can't get rid of her, I will.

December 17th

Mr. Macklin had the nerve to tell me that it was over between us. Ain't that a bitch! Does he think that I am just going to let him go? I won't. No, I can't. I say when it's over. There is no getting rid of Charli. Here it is 2013, and I gave him the best year and a half of my life. He, in turn, filled my life with so much joy, the best dick I ever tasted and had, and now all of a sudden, he wants to end things and make it work with his wife. What kind of woman takes her husband back after she knows that he's in love and is fucking another woman? That is mind boggling to me. Here I am, being loyal and making sure the pussy is only his, and he is chasing behind this backbiting, rat bitch. She is not deserving of a Boss. My heart aches to know that the man I love and would die for is in love with a woman who cannot ever treat him the way I do. She could never love him the way I do. She doesn't get to win. She killed my baby—our baby. The only thing she deserves is misery and death. The more I write, the more jealous rage fills my heart. It is settled. I am getting rid of that bitch and those kids, once and for all.

READING GROUP DISCUSSION QUESTIONS

For Fifty Shades of Trae

1. Do you think Charli is evil? Or simply spoiled, narcissistic, and delusional?

2. In Chinese culture, do you think interracial dating is common?

3. Given the fact that Charli Li is biracial (her mother was Jamaican/her father Chinese), do you think her strong attraction for Trae was because of her own black blood?

4. Why did Charli Li assume Trae would speak Ebonics when she first met him?

5. As an attorney and an heiress to her father's fortune, do you think her status caused Charli Li's brazen behavior toward Trae?

6. Did Trae's affair with Charli Li push Tasha into another man's arms?

7. Was Trae wrong not to want Charli Li's baby when she told him she was pregnant?

8. Do you think Tasha was wrong to push Charli Li

down the stairs, causing her to miscarry her husband's baby?

9. Did Trae develop feelings for Charli Li after her miscarriage? Explain.

10. Why are some women so attracted to married men that they almost develop a fatal attraction for them? Do you think this is what happened to Charli Li?

11. Do you think Charli Li will get revenge on Tasha and her children?

Dear Marvin . . .

By

Kyra Blackshear

Dear Marvin,

I know this letter is long overdue. But things have calmed down for me somewhat, and I'm thinking a little clearer. And now that I'm thinking a little clearer, I have come to grips with the fact that you are gone—my real first childhood sweetheart, the father of my daughter. The love of my life. Yes, I love Rick, but I loved you.

But first, let's talk about our daughter. She misses you very much. When she asks me where you are, I still don't know what to say. I am angry about that. What do I tell her? I haven't figured out how to explain it to her. She's no dummy. She has grown to be smart, inquisitive, and very respectful. She has many of your ways. Trae and Tasha have done an excellent job raising her. They treat her as if she is theirs—so much so that sometimes I feel a little jealous of their relationship.

We are all back on the East Coast. Yeah, go figure. Believe it or not, Tasha was the cause of us having to relocate. Yes, it was that serious. She kick-started a chain of events that landed Trae behind bars and her being hunted down by that Chinese bitch. Kaylin had to step in, and he felt it would be best if he moved us all back East. That way, he could keep an eye on us.

Speaking of Kaylin, he and Angel are doing fine—marriage-wise—for now. The reason I say "for now" is because Angel and Tasha battled long and hard, rallying behind Trae and Kaylin to go legit and stay legit, but now things are looking real suspect. Basically, I'm just sitting back, watching and waiting. If my hunch is right, things are going to get very ugly as the way of life they fought so hard to get away from lands right back in their lap.

And on top of that, Angel wants to leave her husband's law firm and start practicing law with this fine, white guy with a shitload of money. I've never called a white dude fine before. I'm just saying . . .

Now, as for Jaz and Faheem, in my opinion, their lives are a tragedy. That same chick named Oni who came to your house party when Faheem and Jaz were mad at each other, she had a son by him. Yes! You read that right. She gave him a son. But the kicker is, she didn't even tell him. Faheem met his son in a strip mall in the ATL by accident. And get this—the bitch had the nerve to name him Faheem. But then, uniting with his son became bittersweet. Li'l Faheem was kidnapped. When he went to get his son released from the kidnappers, Li'l Faheem got shot and died in his father's arms. It's obvious he can't shake off the fact that he lost his only son. Slowly, he's coming back to the same Faheem that we know. But I have a feeling that when he does, shit's gonna be banannas.

Why do I say that? Because Jaz reminds me of that white chick in *Scandal* who follows Huck around and wants to do what he does. That is Jaz. Having both of them on the same page is *not* a good thing, and you should see them together. They are up to no good.

Okay. I know I've been beating around the bush, talking about everyone and everything else except us. Me and you.

First off, I'm pregnant, Marvin. I'm carrying Rick's

baby. You left him in the trunk of the car. Alive. You missed. Not once. You missed twice. Those drugs caught you slippin'. Now Rick is *still* here. And we are in love.

I admit I made things a bit complicated for Rick. Here I am back in his life, and then I get pregnant. On top of that, I want to spend the rest of my life with him. He wants to spend the rest of his life with me. But then there's Nina, the chick he's engaged to. He feels obligated to her, and he also feels sorry for her. Rick only got with her because she reminded him of me. He thought he had lost me. Thanks to you, he thought I was dead. You left me for dead, *remember*? He thought that I was taken from his life forever. So now he doesn't know how to let her down easy. Looks like I will have to do that for him.

Did you *really* leave me for dead? What did I do to you, Marvin? How could you do something like that to me? I want to know the answer to that so badly. So much so that I tried to find your family and friends at your old hangout spots in hopes of getting some answers. But I couldn't. As soon as Trae found out I was snooping around, he cursed me out and warned me to stop. That's when I knew he had something to do with you not being here.

And then I started to gradually hate him. I tried to get rid of those negative feelings, but they kept getting stronger and stronger, like a root firmly taking hold deep into the earth—like veins in my heart. Trae is my only motivation for writing this letter. I needed to vent. I needed to tell somebody how I feel. I can't tell Tasha. I can't tell Angel, Jaz—nobody. Who can I tell that I hate Trae Macklin?

Honestly, since he broke up my family, I feel that I should break up his.

Shut up, Marvin! I can hear you as if you were here, calling me a hypocrite. I know that's what you are saying. I know you're saying that I am hiding behind Trae. Using him as an excuse.

Maybe I am. But *you* left *me*. Did I still love you? Yes, I did. *Do* I still love you? I still do, even though I'd like to think that I've moved on.

I need closure, Marvin. You haven't given me that. I don't know if I will ever get it.

Kyra

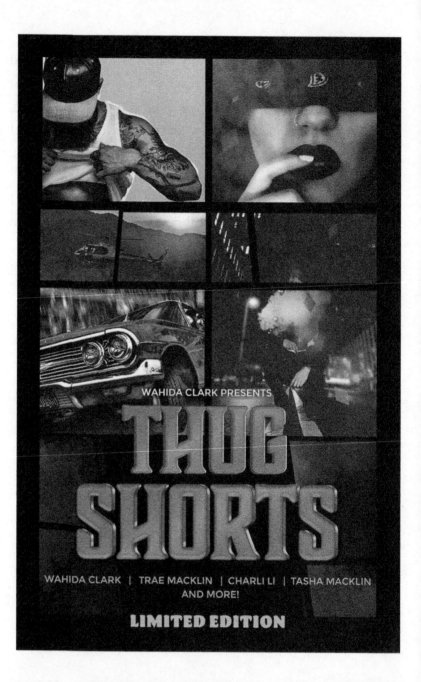

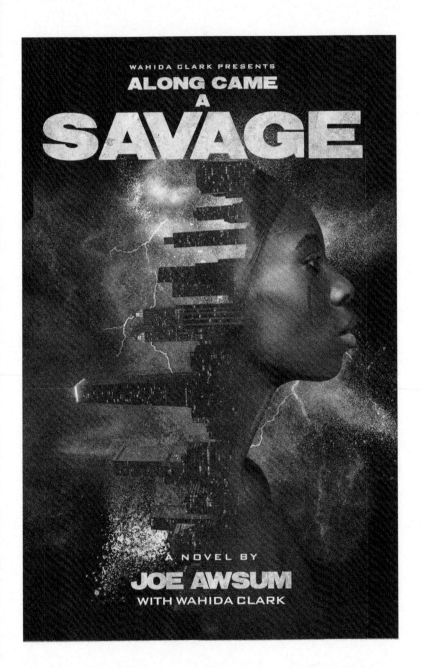

WAHIDA CLARK PRESENTS

ONE LAST DEADLY PLAY

A NOVEL BY
BEST SELLING AUTHOR

FLO ANTHONY

IN STORES NOW

WWW.WCLARKPUBLISHING.COM

IN STORES NOW

CPSIA information can be obtained
at www.ICGtesting.com
Printed in the USA
LVOW03*2344060318
568946LV00004B/29/P